D1927693

Dedicated to Colleen, for being a big inspiration.

Also to Charlie. the best little dog around.

Thank you Colleen for believing in me,
You helped me to write this, you helped it to be.

Thanks also to my mum, I owe you a lot,
and Dad, thanks for giving my book idea a shot.

Woems

AND OTHER SMALL TALES
BY JON THOMPSON

Written and Illustrated
by Jon Thompson

© Copyright 2005 Jon Thompson.
All rights reserved. No part of this publication may be reproduced, stored in a retrieval system, or transmitted, in any form or by any means, electronic, mechanical, photocopying, recording, or otherwise, without the written prior permission of the author.

Note for Librarians: A cataloguing record for this book is available from Library and Archives Canada at www.collectionscanada.ca/amicus/index-e.html
ISBN 1-4120-5590-3

Printed by OCP Limited,
1 Britannia way, Coronation Rd, London NW10 7PW Tel: 0208 965 0921
enquiries@ocpuk.com

TRAFFORD
PUBLISHING™
Offices in Canada, USA, Ireland and UK

This book was published *on-demand* in cooperation with Trafford Publishing. On-demand publishing is a unique process and service of making a book available for retail sale to the public taking advantage of on-demand manufacturing and Internet marketing. On-demand publishing includes promotions, retail sales, manufacturing, order fulfilment, accounting and collecting royalties on behalf of the author.

Book sales for North America and international:
Trafford Publishing, 6E –2333 Government St.,
Victoria, BC V8T 4P4 CANADA
phone 250 383 6864 (toll-free 1 888 232 4444)
fax 250 383 6804; email to orders@trafford.com

Book sales in Europe:
Trafford Publishing (UK) Limited, 9 Park End Street, 2nd Floor
Oxford, UK 0X1 1HH UNITED KINGDOM
phone 44 (0)1865 722 113 (local rate 0845 230 9601)
facsimile 44 (0)1865 722 868; info.uk@trafford.com

Order online at:
trafford.com/05-0488

10 9 8 7 6 5 4 3 2 1

About the Author

Hi, this is Jon Thompson, author and illustrator of Woems.

I am very excited to bring you my first ever (and hopefully not the last!) book. After working on it for so long, there are lots of things running around my mind now it is finally available to you all. Of course I hope that everybody loves it and shows it to their friends and family and they like it and buy it and so on till I am the most famous writer in the world!! But seriously I just want people to enjoy. Its not severe, it's not offensive, but it definitely is me.

So, if you have any views or questions about Woems, I would love for you to get in touch. All web info etc can be found at the back of the book. and I will endeavour to read, reply and throw out where necessary!

Well, enough stalling from me, all that is left to say is... read on!

Best wishes

Jon

Stories

Jerry the Dead

To be a zombie is a terrible fate,
But for Jerry the Dead it's especially great.

He loves to eat brains and wander and moan,
He's empty headed and accident prone.

One day for Jerry he was looking for tea,
When from out of the blue, he walked into a tree.

It knocked him out cold which is bad news for him,
Cos walking behind was a zombie called Tim.

Tim took one look down and went in for a snack,
But was unhappy to see that brains, Jerry lacked.

Good news for Jerry cos Tim couldn't eat him.
Bad news for Tim, it was an unlucky meeting.

Jerry got up and brushed down his robe,
"Sorry 'bout this Tim" and ate his frontal lobe.

Not so jolly Roger

Feel for poor Roger, the pirate with allergies,
Feathers and wood, he can't have either of these.

So bad luck to him when his leg was shot away,
He had a replacement made of sand, rock and clay.

Perhaps even sadder than a man with a leg boulder,
Is the fact the poor guy wanted a bird for his shoulder.

But don't be disheartened, cos one day he espied,
a salesman with a plucked chicken, Rog now wears with pride.

Tommy Gun

The story of Tom is an interesting one,
He's not quite man, he's not quite gun.

Born into a super breed,
A bonny boy they all agreed.

As a kid he trained with blanks,
Readying himself like a two-legged tank.

At age ten he first thwarted evil,
He loaded his head and fired at Man-Weevil.

An overnight star he suddenly became,
For killing a baddie he was highly acclaimed.

For many a year he kept the streets clean,
The bullets were flying, the difference was seen.

But then one day, now a cocky young lad,
Mostly invincible, he couldn't be had.

There was only one weakness for the super hero,
If he sneezed with gun loaded, his brains could blow.

Good for the villains when they discovered the clues,
They called in the Pepper Pot and told him the news.

Pepper was happy cos a condiment man,
Is not that useful in a regular plan.

Of course Tom's time was up when this baddie came,
"Not so special now". they all proclaimed.

Tom couldn't compete, his head would have blew,
Cos guns don't kill pepper... only achoo.

Emma

This is a tale of a very sad girl,
She was thin as paper and as white as a pearl.

The girl in question never laughed or smiled,
No chuckles, no smirks, no grins poor child.

Then one day whilst walking down a dark, creepy path,
For no reason at all she began to laugh.

This carried on for three weeks straight,
Walking down the path, she laughed till late.

Why you may ask was Emma so cheery?
After years and years of being so dreary.

Was it the nice, quiet, refreshing walk?
Perhaps she found a boy to whom she could talk.

No, nothing like that, not for this one,
She simply went crazy, lack of food and the sun.

Now in a home, she still laughs at some things,
But only when all the injections kick in.

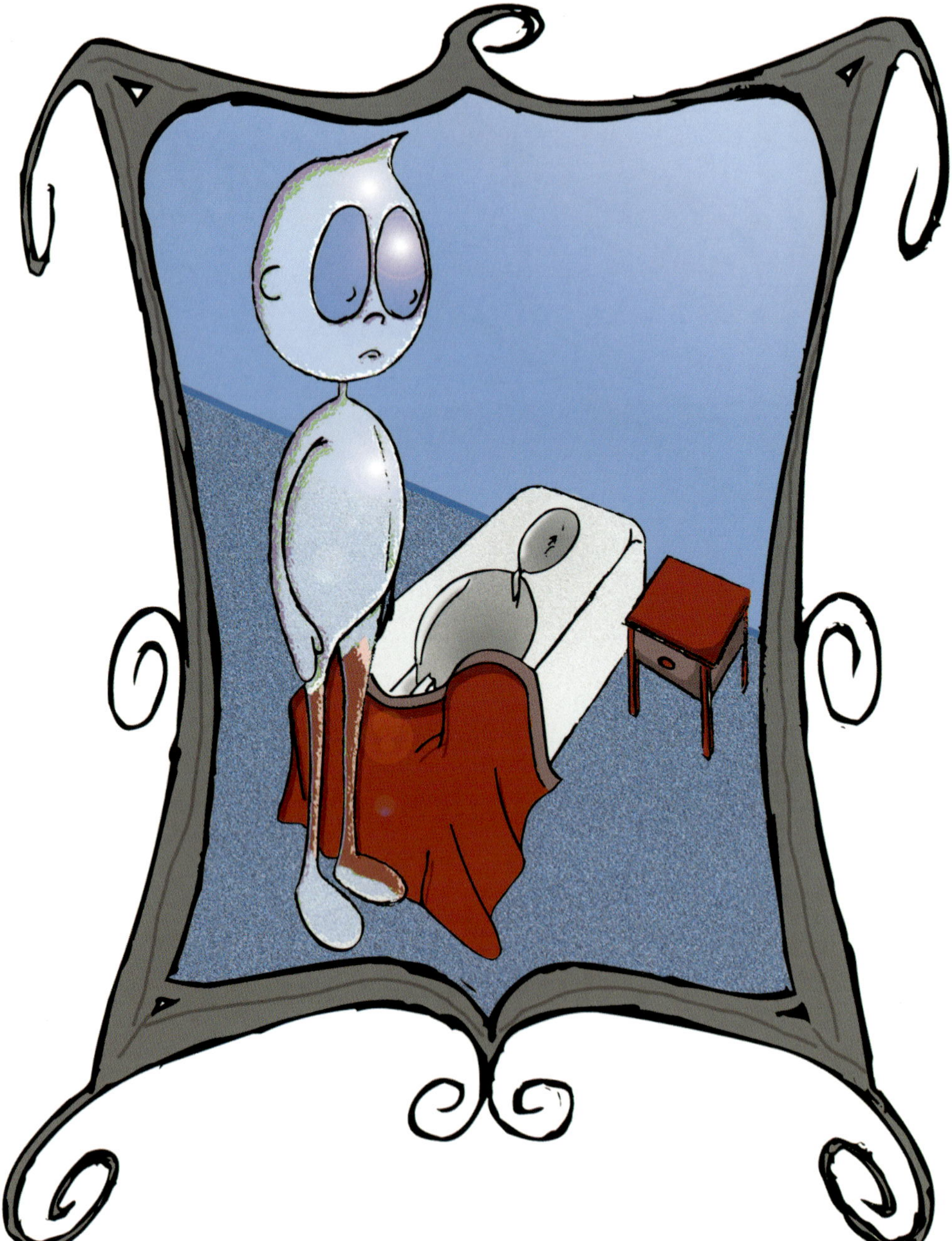

Sleepy Glass

A man made of glass should have plenty of sleep,
Not only for him but also the company he keeps.

Cos one day if he didn't think that sleep really mattered,
He could fall flat on his back and die of being shattered.

An endearing story of a man and a tree

Look at what happened when a man and a tree,
Fell deeply in love, they married at sea.

Perhaps you'd think from stories of old,
That a man/tree combo would sprout a wood child.

But that's not the case in this fateful tale,
Instead they gave birth to a strange young male.

From out of the dirt the one time you'll see,
A living, breathing, skin and bone tree.

Corparlicus the Great

This strange little alien came out of the sky,
His name was Corparlicus and he had just one eye.

He didn't wanna make friends, he just wanted to rule,
The whole point of him coming was to scare all.

He landed in a street, in the centre of Tooting,
Took out his blaster and started shooting.

"Oi, what d'you think you're playin' at?
Show us your face, take off the silly alien hat."

This enraged Corparlicus, he began to shoot some more.
"Cheeky Earth aliens" he thought and let out a great roar.

Now even though he was a superior being,
His only concern was with people fleeing.

Couple this with the fact, he had poor depth perception,
He completely missed the big car coming towards his direction.

SPLAT. That was the end of this alien's God-like vision,
"Henry you old fool, you hit another bloody pigeon"

The Lesser-Known Daw

Hear the cries of the lesser-Known Daw,
So shrill and loud, they deafen us all.

But keep listening on when the sound has stopped,
BANG... like something from the air has dropped.

You see it's a tough life for the flying half-elf,
The sound is so loud, it kills itself.

So next time you hear the rarest of callings,
Don't stop to admire, just beware the Daw falling.

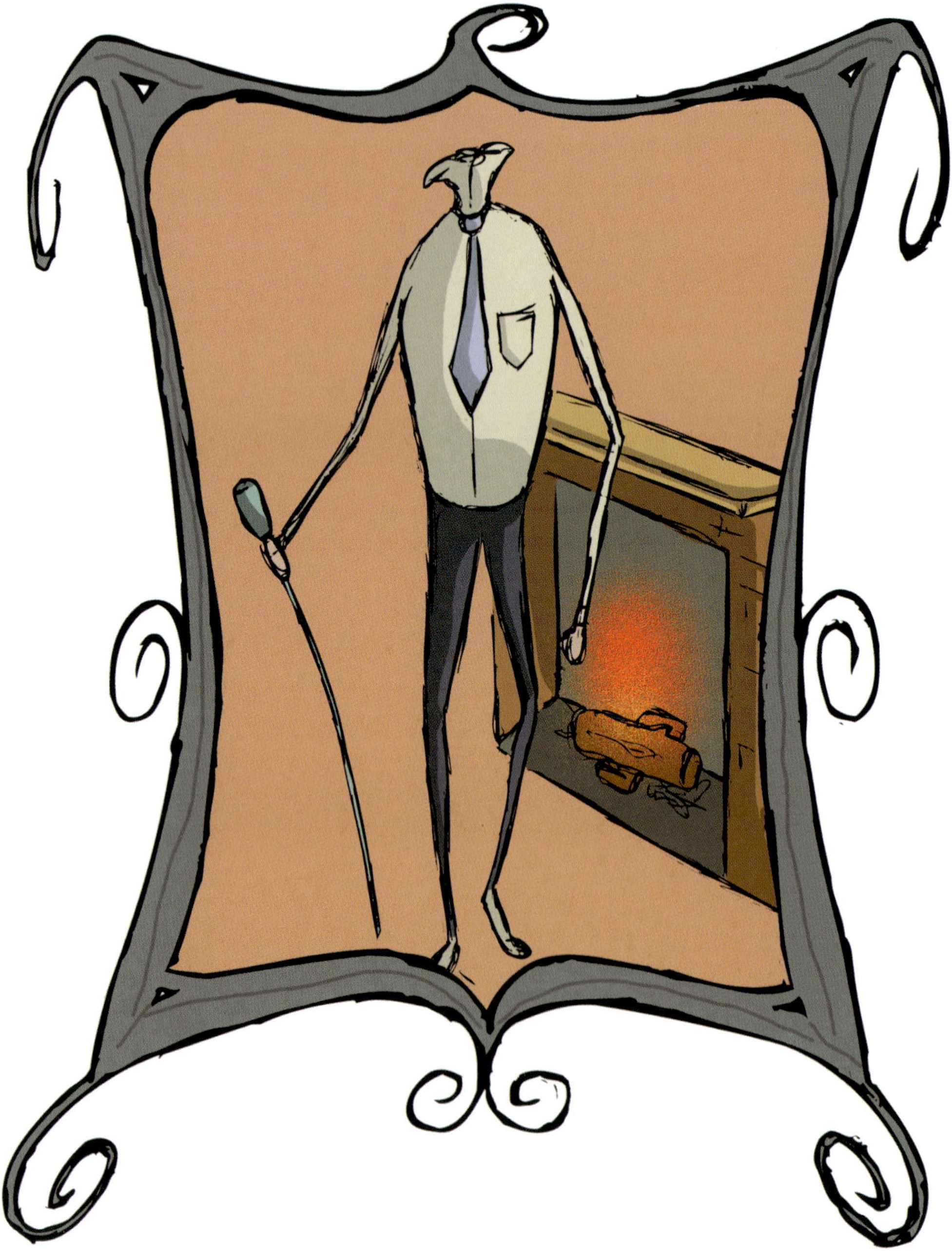

Headless

What can you say about a man with no head?
He never saw daylight, and never ate bread.

But one thing this man can be grateful for,
The cost of his headwear is incredibly small.

WELCOME TO
WANDSHIRE
NO MORTALS!

Welcome to Wandshire

Welcome ye all to Wandshire, the worlds witchiest town,
Where all the witches smile (There is a curse for a frown!)

Ye and I cannot enter, it's for spellcasters alone,
If mortal is caught, they are turned into stone.

They live their own lives here, there are shops of food, clothes and bags,
All owned by the witches, well, the more business-like hags.

There are some male witches, they are called warlocks,
Not so manly though, Wandshire men wear the frocks.

A good little life it is for a witch and her man,
Most just lie in the sun, getting a green tan.

There's a problem though with Wandshire, it's getting too small,
Not over-population, but the growing human-stone wall.

So where lies the solution? They can't let people in,
But the sun-blocker mortals are paling their skin.

"Eureka, I have it!" Said one smelly old crone,
"Why do we not just push it all down?"

So all of the town went to push over the wall,
But they pulled instead and it crushed them all.

Now when ye go to Wandshire, seeking a witch,
Don't look for the man wall, just a big magic ditch.

Poor Cleo

A beautiful girl was Cleo, gorgeous and so sweet,
Such a special person, such a real treat.

But of course a tale being in this book it can't be all nice words,
Cos in fact this girl was so depressed it was bordering on absurd.

She felt the ugly duckling, her mirror showed a lie,
"Everyone is prettier than me, she said with a big sigh."

This was Cleo's downfall, the worry sent her to her grave,
A girl can't live in a world where her confidence is frayed.

But as she walked to the pearly gates, it opened up her eyes,
All the women walking round, she saw they weren't so nice.

Because people in the afterlife don't have expensive skin care,
Everyone looks their real selves in the heavenly air.

So finally she was the swan and could hold her head up high,
"Damn, I wish I'd seen this sooner, I wouldn't have gone and died!"

Michael the Gas Man

Some gas men are not gas men,
Some are men of gas.

This gas man is one of them,
Created by his lass.

She was buying heating with the guy,
And wasn't taking care.

Tripped over trying to swat a fly,
And knocked a gas can in the air.

The canister fell on Mike's head,
And blew up on impact.

Poor old guy, he was dead,
And the fly was still intact.

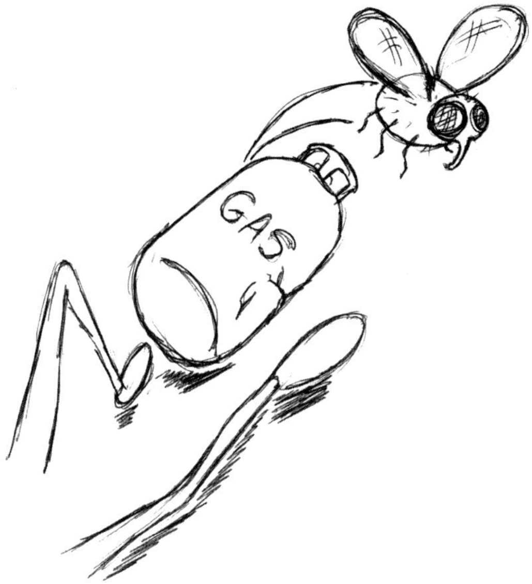
GAS

Instead of resting in the afterlife,
The reaper he stood before.

"You're going back down to the wife,
But now as something more."

We need a superhero there,
And gasman's a cool title.

You will be just and fair,
So go back down now Michael.

Michael could not say more,
This will forever be his rattle.

Unable to walk the heavenly floor,
He's up the creek without a paddle.

So whenever you smell the gassy smell
beware you muggers, killers and cheaters.

The tortured gasman will give you hell,
He's not here to read your meter.

HERE
LIES

Sounds of a tortured soul

Take a look into an old graveyard sight,
A ghostly figure walks the path at night.

Caught in limbo, his soul screams for rest,
A haunted sound howls in from the west.

Tortured to roam the grounds forever more,
The scariest thing you ever saw.

So never go down to this place of unrest,
You will never return, the sight scares you to death.

And the last sound that's heard before you die of the fear,
Is "This ain't fair, I'm not even bloody well buried here!"

10

A flat, paper man?

Imagine of you can, a flat, paper man,
Now imagine if you will, how he ended life in a till.
(If it helps, his name was Bill.)

Mohair Paul

If the thought of itchy jumpers makes your skin crawl,
Imagine what it's like for poor mohair Paul.

Being made of wool is an awful thing to bare,
So horribly itchy, so incredibly rare.

Paul often tries to end his life,
But only unravels if he stabs himself with a knife.

"What's there to live for? Just scratching all day,
The itching's unbearable, it wont go away!"

So on lived our Paul, all threadbare and worn,
Scratching away, wishing he'd never been born.

Tired of life and run out of juice,
He went to a castle and became a recluse.

For the past 40 years he's lived in that place,
No visitors or fun, just wool tears running down his face.

Poor old Paul, will you ever get what you want?
"Not for someone like me, I'm a frayed knot!"

Jeff Round

There was a young man who was as round as a ball,
Couldn't walk far, couldn't stand tall.

Always he wanted to be a sports star,
Have loads of money and expensive cars.

Then one day his dream kinda came true,
A friend said, "We're playing pool, we need you!"

But little did he know, they were only after his size,

Cos Jeff was only 3 inches and they were missing a ❺.

Story of Man-Weevil

Something changed the life of poor Ralph,
Whilst working in cotton fields, in the deep south.

Good young man, hardworking and prim,
Didn't deserve what happened to him.

Toiling in the fields one summers day,
He heard millions of footsteps coming his way.

Before he could say "What on earth's that?"
Thousands of weevils swept over, knocking him flat.

If it couldn't get worse, these weevils were gi-ant,
They came from a disused, leaking, radioactive plant.

Ralph lay helpless on the dirty, wet mud,
"Ouch. one of them bit me, it's drawing blood."

"I feel so weird, like some things happening to me."
He then fell unconscious for days, at least two or three.

When he woke up, he was Ralph no more,
He'd the power of an insect and a new pair of claws.

Full of bitterness and rage at the bite,
The mighty Man-Weevil had risen to fight.

"Hear this to all who live comfortably with bugs,
I will kill you all, you'll be swept under the rug."

With his new powers an evil was unfurled,
Killing innocent people, Weevil ruled the world.

So here ends the tale of how a man can turn bad,
Armed with pure hatred, and of course leather-clad.

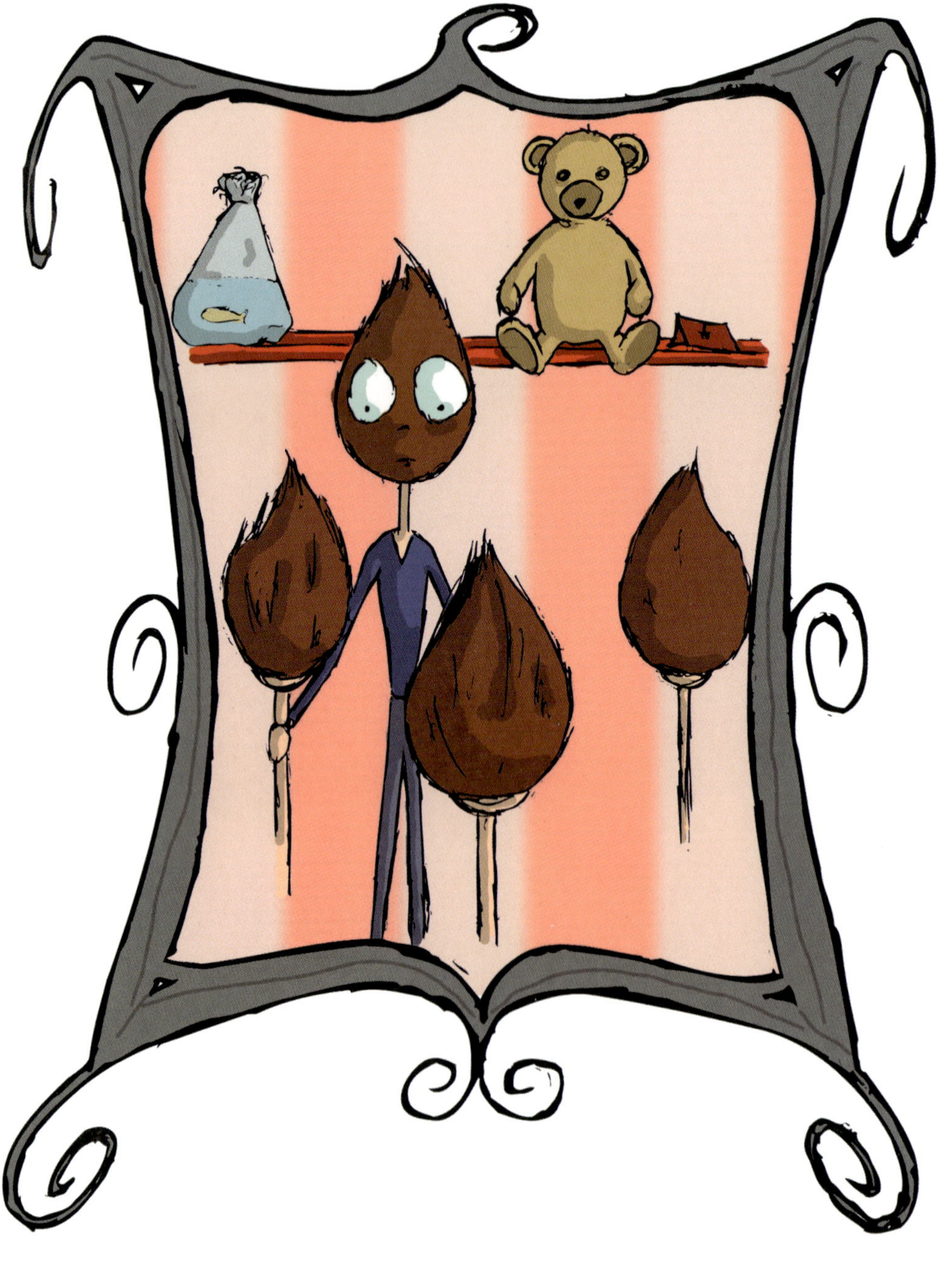

Coconut Boy

Roll up, roll up, roll up - come down to Lando's Fair,
There's lots for you to see and do, some weird and strange or rare.

We have all the usual rides, like the Ghost House and the Wheel,
There's candy floss or toffee apples. Perhaps a goldfish will appeal.

In this particular fun fair, there are oddities to be found,
Like the bearded lady with her son, the boy who's half hound.

And if those things don't freak you out, follow to where few tread,
And come round to the house of the boy with the coconut head.

No-one knows from where he came, people can but guess,
Some think he's a freak of nature, or just a hard-shelled mess.

Why won't he say how he came to be? Laws of nature don't apply.
I guess it's not for us to reason, Coconut Boy's just coconut shy.

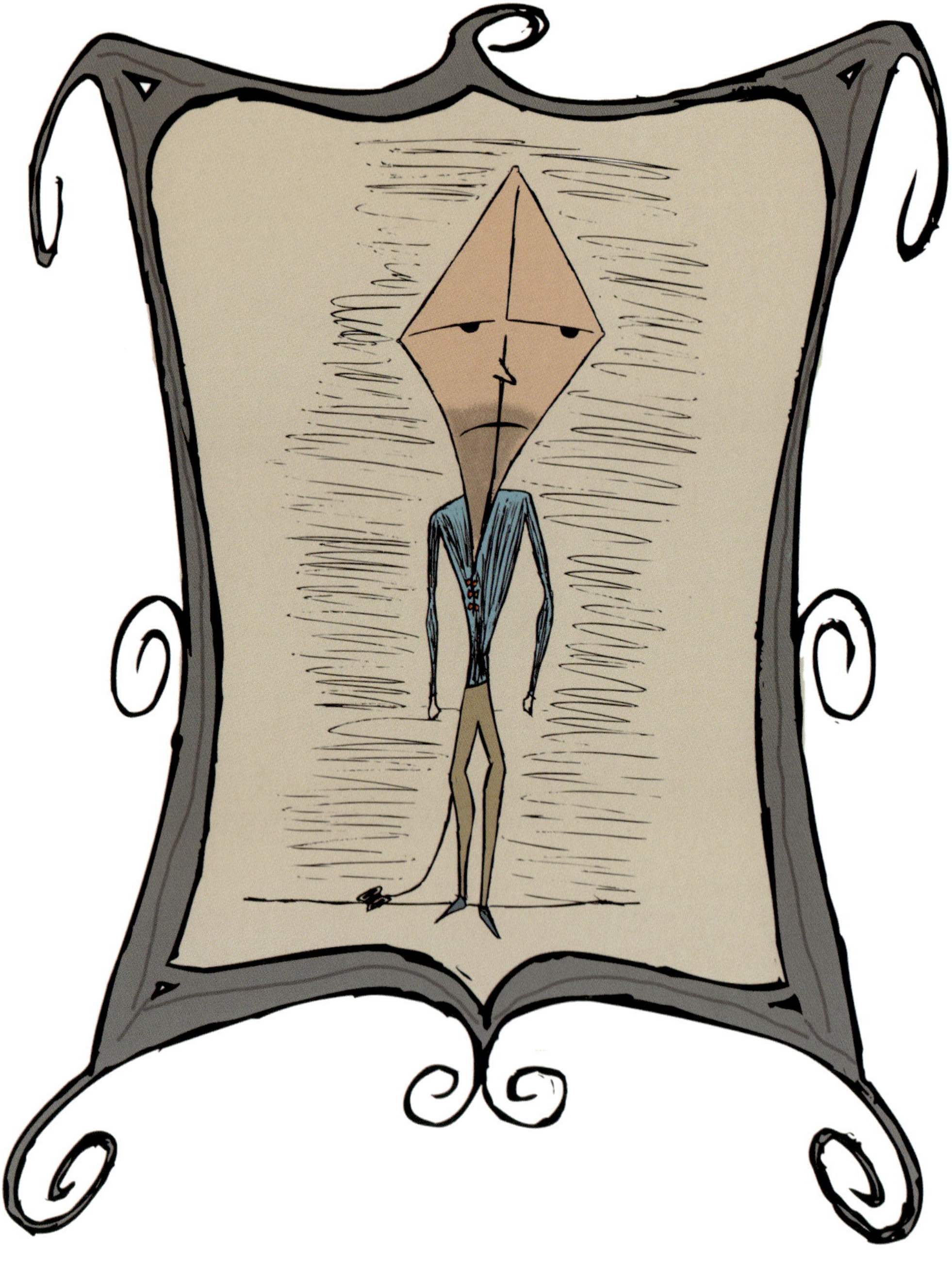

Pete

Poor old Pete born with a head like a kite,
Could only go out on a calm, breezeless night.

But one evening walking whilst out with his mate,
The winds picked up, sealing his fate.

His pal hung onto him as they blew in the breeze,
"What's going on Pete? There's wind up my knees."

Don't worry for them though, it all turns out well,
The winds they were in dropped around the Seychelles.

For more information about Jon, the book, merchandise or upcoming news and information, please log on to:
www.woems.com

Or you can email **info@woems.com**
with any queries or comments you may have for Jon.

These addresses are correct as of September 2005.

First-time author Jon Thompson invites you into this wonderfully dark collection of 'short-story poetry'.

19 grim tales will take your mind on a great journey of life, death, the after-life, and everywhere in-between without so much as a bathroom stop. So relax, get comfy and enter the incredible world of Woems.

ISBN 141205590-3

9 781412 055901